D0512502

BRENT LIBRARIES

Please return/renew this item
by the last date shown.
Books may also be renewed by
phone or online.
Tel: 0115 929 3388
On-line www.brent.gov.uk/libraryservice

templar

9112000127544

A TEMPLAR BOOK

First published in the UK in 2013

by Templar Publishing,

celessence™

Scent technology by Celessence™

First edition

ISBN 978 1 84877 969 3

Printed and bound by CPI Group (UK) Ltd, Croydon, CR0 4YY

Prologue

Our world is only the beginning.
Beneath the surface and between the
moonbeams there is another place.
A place where the flowers sing and
birds and animals live happily with
the little people of Fairyland.

All the magic in our world comes
from this place, through doorways that
only the fairies can open. And, at the

centre of the magic is the Fairythorn Tree.

The Fairythorn, as the little people call it, is always the oldest tree in any garden, wood or park. It might be gnarled and spiky on the outside, but it is a comfortable home for the tiny fairies who live hidden inside its trunk and branches.

And if you look very closely, right down where the base of the trunk meets the mossy ground, you might just spot a doorway to the fairies' world.

Look very closely, now. It's even smaller than you think…

Chapter 1

In the great oak tree at the bottom of the Millers' back garden, a fairy was hard at work. Honeysuckle was putting the finishing touches to her new bedroom, inside one of the uppermost branches of the Fairythorn Tree.

The tree was a very special home to many fairies who lived outside of Fairyland, in the human world, helping to look after nature and wildlife.

Recently, Honeysuckle had been

sharing a room with one of her best friends, Rose. She'd been so upset when one of the humans – or the Bigs, as the fairies called them – had torn off the branch that had housed her bedroom. But at least none of the fairies had been hurt and, although Mr Miller had been threatening to chop down the tree to make way for his new shed, he'd changed his mind.

It had turned out that one of his favourite birds – a Great Spotted Cuckoo – was living in the top of the Fairythorn, which might have had something to do with fairy magic…

Honeysuckle had thought that she'd never love a bedroom like she'd loved her old one, with its ivy-edged window and honeycomb walls, but as she spun around she had to admit that this one looked pretty good.

She shook out the patchwork petal duvet on top of her new scallop-shell bed, and then skipped over to the pine-cone rocking chair that Posy had made especially for her. But Honeysuckle was too excited to sit down now she had a bedroom to herself once again.

She'd had fun sharing a room,

and Rose's large bedroom in one of the lower branches was perfectly big enough, but Honeysuckle liked to sit alone and daydream – and you can't really do that with a room-mate watching!

She picked up a pearl pinhead that was resting against the wall, and bounced over to the arched oak door that led to the corridor beyond. As she pushed her new pearl doorknob into place, she could hear whistling and singing and quite a lot of banging. The other fairies who'd lost everything when the branch had been torn off were busy moving into their new bedrooms, too.

Honeysuckle twirled back round and grinned at the gleaming beeswax walls and the soft and spongy moss-pile floor. She felt so lucky that her four best friends had helped her decorate – and now, her bedroom was ready!

Her dragling, Pip, nudged her knee and Honeysuckle bent down to rub Pip's green, furry nose. Every fairy had a dragling as a companion, and whilst they could sometimes be a bit naughty, they were also adorable.

Pip mewled at Honeysuckle as she tickled the underside of her chin. Her tail flicked about contently and brushed Honeysuckle's brand-new ballet shoes that were hanging on the wall. When Honeysuckle had lost her beloved old pair in the broken tree branch, Fleur had made her these new ones as a surprise.

Honeysuckle reached over to steady the shoes as they swung on their hook next to the knothole window. As she did so, something outside caught her eye. It was her three best friends playing fairy bungee on a long, wide branch just above the window, their wings sparkling in the light from the crescent moon.

She watched as they all jumped from the branch at the same time, diving down as far as they dared and then frantically flapping their wings to rise up before they hit the ground. Fleur almost always won – she was the biggest daredevil of them all.

As they flew back to the branch for another go, giggling and squealing, Honeysuckle felt her mouth droop. Her wings had yet to unfurl, and until they did, she couldn't join in with the game.

She had never really been worried about her wings before, but now all her best friends had theirs she couldn't help feeling a bit left out. Not that they meant her to feel bad –

earlier today Rose had suggested that she could join in by riding on the back of a swallow, but Honeysuckle knew it wouldn't be the same.

She rested her elbows on the window ledge and sighed. She had always liked spending a bit of time on her own, but she was starting to feel fed up. Then she had a terrible thought. What if she was the first fairy never to get her wings? That would be dreadful!

A fairy's wings unfurled when the fairy discovered her purpose in life – Rose was a Wish Fairy, Posy a Dragling Fairy and Fleur a Song Fairy – but what if Honeysuckle never found her purpose?

Crash! A noise from behind Honeysuckle made her jump in fright. She spun round and saw her new bottle-top mirror lying on the mossy floor. How in Fairyland had that happened? She knew she could be rather clumsy, but she hadn't been anywhere near the mirror, which hung to the right of the door. It wasn't Pip either – she was gently snoring away on her dandelion-head bed in the corner of the room.

Honeysuckle rushed over to pick up the mirror, and let out a sigh of relief when she saw it hadn't broken. The last thing she needed was seven years' bad luck!

She carefully nestled the shiny round mirror back on its hook and as she did so, her long blonde hair whipped about her face. A strong breeze was blowing about her room. Was that what had knocked down the mirror? It hadn't been at all windy earlier that day, she remembered. It had been very hot, the air humid and still, and the garden gnomes, Clive and Derek, had been complaining.

"Inside, quickly!" Honeysuckle heard someone shout. She ran over to the window and felt a great blast of air whoosh past as she stuck her head out. The leaves on the Fairythorn Tree were blowing about crazily, and the fairies outside were all rushing towards the tiny doorway at the bottom of the trunk.

A storm was coming!

Chapter 2

"Grow a leaf, grow a leaf, Fairythorn Tree," sang Rose.

"Grow lots of leaves, as fast as can be," Fleur replied, clapping her hands against Rose's in time with the song.

Honeysuckle, Rose, Fleur and Posy were all huddled inside Honeysuckle's bedroom, waiting for the storm to pass. Rose and Fleur were sitting on the mossy rug with their legs crossed, their singing drowning out the swirling wind and the creaking groans of the Fairythorn Tree as the gale outside continued.

On the other side of the room, Posy was showing Honeysuckle how to make a feather headdress. Posy was wonderful at making things, especially headdresses. Today she was wearing one made from feathers that she'd found in the garden and dyed purple with berry juice. It matched her stunning peacock-like wings perfectly.

"So you just grasp the ends together," Posy said, holding out the golden feathers that Honeysuckle had collected, "and tie them tightly, just like this."

Honeysuckle tried to copy exactly what Posy was doing, but as she twisted the spider-web silk around the ends of the feathers, she got her hands in a muddle and dropped the whole lot.

"Bother!" she cried, and then smiled up at Posy and winked. "I think I might leave making things to you!"

With her friends all around her, Honeysuckle was feeling a lot better. And she didn't mind not being very good at crafts – Posy was the one who could make an amazing new outfit just from bits and pieces she found around the garden, whereas Honeysuckle was good at other things, like dancing.

She wondered when she'd next be able to get outside to practise – the storm didn't look as if it would be stopping any time soon.

"How are things going with the draglings?" Honeysuckle asked Posy. As a Dragling Fairy, Posy trained the little creatures, and sometimes this could be a bit tricky. The draglings protected their fairies fiercely, but they could also be quite naughty.

"Not too bad thanks," Posy replied. "Although one of them did tread on an ants' nest last week, and we had to spend the rest of the day rebuilding it. Gruff didn't mean to, of course, but he's really quite clumsy."

Honeysuckle grinned – she knew how that felt! She glanced over at Pip, who was playing with her friends' draglings on her bed. They were getting tangled up in the covers and mewling with delight. Sometimes Honeysuckle wished that she could understand dragling language, like Posy could, but she was so close to Pip she often thought she knew what she was thinking anyway.

Rose and Fleur had finished their game and were now both peeking through the nettle-green spider-silk curtains at the window.

"I wonder how the animals are doing outside," said Rose, rubbing her forehead and frowning. "I hope they've found shelter all right."

"Are you sure you can't do a wish, to make sure they're okay?" Fleur asked. The wind from outside was making the tiny stars in her red curls spin and sparkle.

Rose shook her head. "Wish Fairies can only grant the wishes of Bigs – not our own or those from other fairies," she said. "But it's so dreadful out there, I feel terrible not being able to help."

"Hopefully it'll calm down soon," said Honeysuckle, as she passed another bunch of golden feathers to Posy. "Then we can go and check on everyone."

Posy nodded. "The Cloud Fairies will make sure it's better by the morning."

At that moment, a large leaf flew up against the window, flapping wildly. Rose and Fleur both jumped back.

"But what if it isn't better?" Rose said. "What if it gets worse? The Fairythorn Tree could be in danger."

Honeysuckle gasped. Rose had a point. The tree was very, very old, and it was doing a lot of creaking in the wind. They couldn't lose their home – not just a few days after saving it from Mr Miller's axe!

The friends looked at each other, eyes wide.

"I'm sorry, everyone," said Rose. "I'm just worrying too much. I'm sure the tree will be fine." She slumped to the floor and leaned against the shimmering beeswax wall.

"I guess I should go to bed," said Fleur, heading for the door. "I'll be yawning my way through tomorrow's Sunrise Song otherwise."

She called to her dragling, Red, and he scampered to her side.

It was way past their usual bedtime, Honeysuckle realised. But with the wind howling outside, and the thought of the Fairythorn Tree in danger again, she wondered how she'd ever be able to sleep.

Chapter 3

Honeysuckle rubbed the sleep from her eyes. She must have nodded off after all last night – it was light in her room, which must mean it was after dawn. She jumped out of her scallop-shell bed and ran over to the window.

Her heart leapt in relief – the garden was peaceful once more and the storm was clearly over. She could see some fairies flying about the garden already – checking up on the animals and wildlife, no doubt.

Rap, rap! came a tap on her door.

"Honeysuckle? Are you awake?" a voice called.

"Yes, come in!" Honeysuckle replied.

Fleur poked her head around the door and Red's nose appeared below it. "I'm just back from the Sunrise Song," she said. "But I'm going out again to help with the garden clean-up. Are you coming?"

Honeysuckle nodded. "I'll meet you by the pond in five minutes."

Fleur's head disappeared again

and Honeysuckle quickly got dressed. She usually liked to wear a silk layered tutu, but today she pulled on mint-leaf leggings and a floaty daisy-petal top, in case there was a lot of work to do.

Soon Honeysuckle and Pip were rushing down the Fairythorn Tree's central spiral staircase. The walls were covered in 'shiny bits' that the fairies had collected from the Bigs' garden. Many other fairies were going up and down the steps, and it took Honeysuckle longer than usual to get to the ground and pop out of the tiny Fairythorn door at the bottom.

She glanced about her and whistled to a passing dragonfly. She was soon nestled on his back and whizzing towards the pond, with Pip flying close behind her. As they went, Honeysuckle took in the garden – there were a few fallen flower pots here and there, but it really wasn't as bad as she'd thought it would be.

They reached the pond and Fleur slid down from the dragonfly's back. "Thank you," she said, as it rose up into the air once again.

On the cracked flagstones that surrounded the pond, Fleur, Posy and Rose were picking up lost lily pads that had blown out of the water and scattered everywhere.

"Hi, Honeysuckle!" Posy called. "Isn't it great that everything is okay?"

"There are a few things to tidy up," Rose said as she peeled a wet lily pad from the paving. "But I thought it would be so much worse."

"I don't know what you're so pleased about, pea-brain," one of the grumpy garden gnomes interrupted.

It was Clive, Honeysuckle realised – though she could only tell the two identical gnomes apart by the crack in Clive's hat.

"Nasty wind," Clive whined. "Gave me awful earache, it did."

"Not as bad as mine!" the other gnome, Derek, joined in. "At least you were sheltered behind me. The storm was so strong I thought my beard would be blown off."

Honeysuckle stifled a giggle.

Their long white beards were painted on – there was no chance of them blowing anywhere!

The four friends ignored the moaning gnomes.

"Got to dash," Posy said. "I'm doing Advanced Fairy Defence with the draglings today."

It was important that the draglings protected their fairies, especially from the nasty Grot Goblins who liked to ruin nature wherever they could. The fairies rarely saw the them, but the goblins were attracted by pollution and so, they were turning up more and more in the Bigs' world.

"I'm on my way, too." Rose was already rising up above Honeysuckle. "There's a meeting for the Wish Fairies this morning in the Fairythorn Tree."

"Ooh, I almost forgot." Fleur clapped a hand to her mouth. "I've got practice for the full moon concert today. You'll be okay, won't you, Honeysuckle?"

"Of course," Honeysuckle said, waving them away. "See you later!"

As her friends and their draglings fluttered off, Honeysuckle glanced up at the sun that had just appeared from behind a fluffy white cloud. It was hard to believe there'd been such a big storm last night.

She wandered away from the pond and onto the lawn, with Pip skipping around her. Honeysuckle would usually dance around too, jumping between the grasses with the bees and other insects. But she didn't feel much like doing that today, and there weren't many insects about anyway. *Perhaps they're all still sheltering after last night*, she thought.

She pushed her way through

the grass that rose up like curtains – it was much longer than usual. Mr Miller must be away. He usually cut it every couple of days, much to Clive and Derek's disgust – they always complained that the little bits of cut grass tickled them.

"Eeek! Aaagh!"

Honeysuckle tipped her head up at the sound from the Bigs' back door. She stood on tiptoes to see above the lawn. The little Big, Alice, was doing some kind of dance, shaking her head to the right and then to the left. She flapped her hands up and hopped from one leg to the other. *The Bigs do dance funnily*, thought Honeysuckle.

Alice hopped closer, and Honeysuckle realised what was going on. The little Big wasn't dancing – she had a bee buzzing around her head! But that was odd – the bees were usually so well behaved. And this was pollination season. They should all be very busy, carrying pollen between the flowers and plants.

As Alice jumped and squealed, Honeysuckle had a sudden thought. This was the first bee she'd seen all day. That was weird – lots of bees lived in their nest in the Fairythorn Tree, and she saw them all the time.

"Go away, bee!" the little Big squeaked, spinning round on the spot. The bee bumped into Alice's long hair, and then fell away again. The little Big took her chance and darted back into the kitchen, slamming the door shut behind her. Honeysuckle rushed over to where the bee had tumbled.

She was out of breath by the time she'd waded through the long grass to reach the little insect. The bee lay still, but her eyes were open and her wings flickered.

Honeysuckle knelt down next to the bee and in a very soft voice, asked, "Are you okay?"

The bee buzzed gently and then jolted up. "Huh…yes, no…pardon?" she said in a high-pitched, vibrating hum.

"What's the matter, little bee?" Honeysuckle said. "Why aren't you pollinating?"

The bee gave a deep buzz of her wings and suddenly spun upwards. "Can't... who... what... where am I?"

Before Honeysuckle could reply, the bee had sped away, looking dazed and confused. *The poor bee*, Honeysuckle thought. *What in Fairyland's going on?*

Chapter 4

Honeysuckle clasped her hands together as she watched the bee dart off. What should she do? She was very fond of the bees, and although they worked extremely hard and didn't have much time for anyone else, they would usually stop to say hello to her.

She thought they were amazing – helping nature to grow by pollinating the plants and flowers, and making masses of delicious honey. Not to mention the beautiful beeswax that she'd used to decorate her bedroom walls.

As Honeysuckle wondered what to do, she noticed a spark of light next to the trunk of the tree. Her mouth dropped open. It was a bright, glowing ball, bobbing in the air like a low-hanging moon. Honeysuckle knew what it meant – Mother Nature was on her way!

Honeysuckle had to get back to the tree, and quickly. She waved both arms at a passing Orange-tip butterfly, but at first Honeysuckle thought it hadn't seen her. Then the butterfly came to an abrupt stop, turned in the air, and flew back.

"Thanks!" Honeysuckle cried. "I have to get back for Mother Nature."

"I don't know why you couldn't ask someone else," the butterfly said. "I'm in a rush too, you know."

"Please?" said Honeysuckle. She knew it must be something important if Mother Nature herself had come – usually she sent messages to the fairies by butterflies or fireflies.

The butterfly huffed and fluttered her orange-tipped wings. "All right," she agreed. "I suppose I've no choice. But hurry up!"

Honeysuckle pulled herself on to the butterfly's yellow back and held on tight. She knew not to worry about its bad mood – despite their incredible beauty, butterflies were known for being grumpy. If it wasn't an emergency, she would have looked around for someone else to help her. If only she had her wings – then she'd never have this problem again!

By the time Honeysuckle and Pip had arrived at the foot of the Fairythorn Tree, Mother Nature had appeared in her full form. The glowing ball of light had been replaced by a beautiful woman, who seemed to glimmer and sparkle in the sun. She had skin as white as milk, and sea-green eyes.

Nestled on top of her wavy chestnut hair was a grand crown made of gorgeous multi-coloured flowers.

"Fairy friends," Mother Nature began, her voice deep and her face still. "I'm afraid I'm here with bad news."

A wave of concerned whispers started up among the fairies who'd all gathered around the tree.

Mother Nature held up her hand for quiet. The fairies were silent once again. "I'm sorry to say that last night's storm wasn't just bad weather. My messengers tell me that it was the Grot Goblins, who decided to make trouble in the local farmer's fields."

Honeysuckle shivered. What had the Grot Goblins been up to? This didn't sound good.

"They created a giant wind to blow the spray the farmers use on their crops away from the fields and into the local gardens," she continued. "That was what the storm was – the Grot Goblins blasting the air everywhere."

Honeysuckle caught Rose's eye. Her fairy friend looked as worried as she felt. The farmers' sprays could be bad for wildlife, and sometimes even poisonous.

"The problem is, the spray seems to be affecting the bees," Mother Nature went on. "It's making them woozy and confused, and they are forgetting to eat, and where their nest is. There are a lot of lost and hungry bees about."

As Mother Nature spoke, Honeysuckle spotted a bee near the flower beds, buzzing in a slow circle, and another one diving towards the patio and then flying back again, like a boomerang.

So that was it! Honeysuckle thought. It all made sense now. Her heart sank. The bees must feel awful, being dazed and not knowing what was going on.

"As you all know, fairies," Mother Nature said, "this is a very important time for pollination. With the bees out of action, I need everyone's help to pollinate the plants and flowers. Pollen Fairies, please show the others what they need to do. I'm going to ask the dragonflies, butterflies and other flying insects to help out too."

Mother Nature paused for a moment as she looked around at the crowd. "It's important you all get started right away – we're already very behind."

The Pollen Fairies began flying off. Many of the other fairies followed, offering their help. Honeysuckle rushed over to Rose, and Fleur and Posy joined them too.

But Mother Nature had not yet gone. "Honeysuckle," she called. "Can I ask a special favour?"

Honeysuckle glanced up, surprised. "Yes, of course, Mother Nature," she said.

"Good." Mother Nature's green eyes looked deep into Honeysuckle's blue ones. "I worry that there aren't enough fairies to do the job of the bees, and the other insects aren't used to such intensive work. You're so good at dancing between the plants and flowers – will you guide your friends so they can help out in this time of need?"

Honeysuckle felt honoured, but also a little nervous. Would she really be able to do anything useful to help?

Rose nudged her, and she realised she needed to say something. Honeysuckle looked up at Mother Nature's kind face. "Yes," she whispered. "I'll try my very best."

Mother Nature gave Honeysuckle a small smile. "Then it's time for me to go. Thank you, fairies, and good luck!"

The shimmering Mother Nature suddenly shrank back into the golden ball once more, and then, as quickly as it had appeared, the ball exploded into thousands of tiny stars.

Honeysuckle turned to her friends. "We can start at the wildflower patch," she said, pointing behind the Fairythorn Tree to the sprawling mass of flowers. "Let's go!"

Chapter 5

Honeysuckle plucked the pollen from the centre of a bright red poppy and placed it gently into her woven straw basket. It was her fourth basket of the day, and she was feeling pretty tired. Her back ached and her feet were sore, but she knew she couldn't stop – not until sunset at least.

They'd been very busy in the wildflower patch and Posy and Fleur had now gone to help in one of the flower beds.

She moved on to the next flower – a buttercup – and then called to Rose, who was collecting alongside her. "My basket's full. Shall we go and deliver them?"

Rose was fluttering above a long pink foxglove. "Yes, mine's almost full too." She scooped up a handful of foxglove pollen and sprinkled it into her basket.

The two fairies were soon

striding up the path, with Pip and Pax scampering alongside them. It had been very quiet in the garden today – everyone was working too hard to chatter much. But as they approached the pond Honeysuckle could hear shouts and then squeals, and then shouts again.

As they turned the corner, past the purple hydrangea bush, they came upon an unusual sight.

Clive and Derek were standing there, but the fairies could hardly see them. They were covered in butterflies from head to toe!

"Get OFF!" Derek cried. "Hee hee, stop it!"

"Find somewhere else to sit, you gutterflies" Clive moaned. "Eeee, not there, eeeeeee!"

Honeysuckle and Rose burst out laughing. Not only were Clive and Derek hidden by butterflies, it sounded like they were very ticklish, too. The colourful insects were flitting and sitting,

flitting and sitting on the gnomes. Despite being cross, the gnomes were also giggling because the butterflies' wings and feet tickled!

"Go and – eeeeee – protest somewhere else, you creepy caterpillars!" said Derek.

"Yeah, gnomes are not for sitting on – hee hee!" said Clive. "Fairies, do something!"

Honeysuckle had been bent over with laughter, but quickly straightened up and skipped closer to the gnomes. Rose flew along beside her. "What did you say about protesting?"

Honeysuckle asked.

"We're fed up," said one of the butterflies. It looked like the Orange-tip who'd reluctantly given Honeysuckle a lift earlier. "We can't be expected to do all this pollination, just because the bees are suddenly too lazy."

"Yes, it's not fair," said a White Admiral butterfly. "So we're on strike!"

"I don't know why you bigwings have to go on strike here," said Clive. "Stupid butterflies – argh, hee hee!"

Honeysuckle grabbed Rose's arm. "If the butterflies are on strike," she said, "we'll never get all the pollination done!"

Rose's big brown eyes widened at her friend. "You're right, Honeysuckle, this is really bad."

Rose turned to the butterflies. "You shouldn't be protesting," she said. "We need your help with the pollinating. It's not the bees' fault that they're confused."

"More like they'll use any excuse not to work hard," said the White Admiral. "The bees were fine yesterday."

"But it was the Grot Goblins, and

the farmer's spray," Rose said, trying to reason with the grumpy butterflies. "Mother Nature must have told y—"

Rose didn't get the chance to finish her sentence, as the Bigs' back door banged open, and one of the Bigs — Alice's mum — burst outside. In one hand she grasped a mug with 'World's Best Mum' written on it, and she held a newspaper on top of the mug with the other hand. The fairies and their draglings ducked behind the hydrangea bush, out of sight.

With a little shriek, Mrs Miller lifted the newspaper and shook the

mug into the garden… and out flew a bee!

"M u m, what's the matter?" Alice had appeared at the door, her best friend Edie behind her.

"I keep finding bees all around the house!" the Big squealed. "There was one in the shower this morning, and another buzzing inside the airing cupboard. I'd just sat down to have a

cup of coffee and read the paper, and this one fell into my mug!"

"But where have they come from, Mrs Miller?" asked Edie.

"I have no idea," Alice's mum said. "But they won't be staying for long. I hate bees!"

"But, Mum, bees are good – they won't hurt you unless you hurt them," said Alice, slipping on her flip-flops and joining her mum in the garden.

"I just don't like them!" said Mrs Miller. "When I was about your age I stood on a bee and got stung. It really hurt! We can't have them in the house." She jumped as another bee zoomed past her left shoulder. "With your dad away at the conference I'll just have call pest control. I'll get them over in the morning."

Alice's face fell. "Mum, you can't do that!"

"Alice, I've made up my mind," Mrs Miller said. "Now go back in and shut the door, before any more get inside!"

As the Bigs disappeared into the kitchen Honeysuckle started shaking. The bees were in terrible danger!

Chapter 6

Rose and Honeysuckle ran back across the flagstones. The butterflies had stopped flittering around so much, although Clive and Derek were still covered in them.

"Oi, Butterfleas!" Derek said. "We're not your personal sofas, you know."

"This is worse than the ant infestation last year," Clive said. "At least ants have proper jobs to do, carrying things and stuff. Not like you lazy bird wannabes."

"Okay, that's it, I've had enough," said the Orange-tip butterfly. "Pollination is better than listening to you two. We'll leave you horrible lumps of concrete alone." She fluttered up above the pond and beckoned with one wing to the others.

In a blast of rainbow colours, the butterflies took off and swirled up together as one. They looked like a cloud of confetti against the bright blue sky.

Honeysuckle watched the display

for a moment. *That was surprising,* she thought. Clive and Derek had outgrumped the butterflies, and they were finally joining in the pollinating again.

"At least that's one problem solved," she said to Rose.

"True," Rose said. "But what are we going to do about the bees?"

Just then, the kitchen door opened and shut quickly. Alice and Edie had slipped out into the garden. Alice held a box of biscuits and two plastic cups of drink, and Edie was dragging a blanket. The fairies jumped behind

Derek to hide. He grumbled quietly, but knew not to make a scene with the Bigs in the garden.

Honeysuckle peered round Derek's painted body. The little Bigs were shaking out their red tartan blanket on the grass. Then they bounced down on top of it, trying not to spill their drinks.

"There's another bee," Edie said to Alice. It was crawling around the edge of the blanket.

"And there's one more!" Alice said, pointing to a bee that buzzed around a cluster of daisies. "I wonder what's up with them?"

"I don't know." Edie's wild black hair swung around as she shook her head.

Alice's hazel eyes suddenly lit up. "Maybe the fairies will help them!" she said. "Although we haven't seen any for a while."

Alice had first seen a fairy when

Rose had helped her make friends with Edie. The fairies weren't meant to show themselves to Bigs, not really, but Alice and Edie had seen them a couple of times now.

Honeysuckle pulled her head back in behind Derek. "Perhaps they'll make a wish to save the bees," she whispered to Rose. "And then you'll be able to grant it."

"Ooh, I do hope so!" Rose said, clapping her hands together.

"We have to stop Mum somehow," Alice was saying, as the fairies poked their heads back out. "I know she's scared of bees, but they don't mean to frighten her."

"But she said the pest control people will be around in the morning," said Edie. "We haven't got long to make her change her mind!"

As the little Bigs talked, Honeysuckle could feel her hope fading. They hadn't mentioned anything about a wish. She nudged Rose's elbow. "Maybe *we* should ask for *their* help," she said. "Just this once?"

Rose shook her head. "We can't do that – you know we're not meant to unless it's an emergency."

"But this IS an emergency!" Honeysuckle cried, her face hot with worry. "Please, Rose?"

But before the fairy could reply, the scared-of-bees Big shouted through a tiny gap in the back door. "Alice, come and help me with dinner please. Edie, would you like to stay for food?"

"No thanks, Mrs Miller," Edie called back. "Dad's cooking tonight – I'd better head home!"

Edie ran over to the hydrangea bush and scrambled in among the branches. Below the ground was a secret tunnel that connected Alice's and Edie's garden. The fairies had dug it when they'd helped the two little Bigs to make friends.

"Bye, Edie." Alice waved and then folded up the blanket and stacked the plastic cups.

As soon as the little Bigs had gone, the fairies emerged from their hiding place, and Clive and Derek started muttering.

"I still say it's a giant's comb," said Clive.

"Don't be ridiculous – it's a fierce

weapon for a brave knight," Derek replied.

Honeysuckle sighed. They were arguing about the rake that leaned against the back of the house – again. It was their favourite argument. But there was no time to waste listening to them squabble. The fairies had the bees to worry about.

"Look, there's Fleur and Posy!" Rose was pointing at the sky while shielding her eyes from the summer sun. "I'll go and see how they're doing. Will you be okay by yourself for a while, Honeysuckle?"

"Yes, you go," Honeysuckle said, giving her friend a small smile. But as the three fairies and their draglings fluttered away, Honeysuckle sank down onto the flagstones. She should be helping with the pollination, just as she'd been asked, but Honeysuckle figured Mother Nature would be even more upset if the Bigs got rid of the bees.

She squeezed her knees into her chest and took in a deep breath of mint from her leggings. She suddenly felt really alone. Mother Nature had especially asked for her help, but now things had got even worse.

Then it came to her and she jumped up from the ground like a rocket. There was nothing else for it, she realised.

She had to go to Fairyland and find Mother Nature.

Chapter 7

First things first, Honeysuckle had to get back to the Fairythorn Tree. Any fairy could go to Fairyland just by making a simple wish, but they had to be close to a Fairythorn Tree when they made it.

Honeysuckle ran away from the pond and looked about the garden frantically. She couldn't see any birds or butterflies about – they were probably all helping with the pollination. Just

when it looked like she'd have to sprint back through the grass – *and springtime knew how long that would take*, she thought – she spotted a large ant family walking along the path nearby. "Let's go," she called to Pip. "There's no time to waste!"

Soon, Honeysuckle was perched on the back of the army of ants, with Pip flying just above them. Honeysuckle marvelled at how quickly the ants could move – she'd be back at the Fairythorn in no time. They must have been super-strong in order to carry her, but they didn't

seem to mind. She made a mental note to mention their kindness to Mother Nature when she found her.

In the shadow of the Fairythorn Tree, Honeysuckle stepped off the ants. "Thank you so much, ants," she said. "You've done me a huge favour." The ants waved goodbye and got back into army formation, ready to continue their journey.

Honeysuckle stood beneath the Fairythorn branches. Pip waited patiently at her ankles. For a moment, Honeysuckle hoped more than anything that one of her friends would fly by, and she could ask them to come with her. But none of them did. She was on her own.

She crouched down and wrapped an arm around Pip's light-green neck, then squeezed her eyes shut. *I wish to go to Fairyland,* she said in her head. *Please!* she added at the last minute.

Honeysuckle knew she should be used to travelling back and forth to Fairyland, but it was still a wonderful feeling. It was like she was on an invisible, ever-rising roundabout, spinning gently, higher and higher. She opened her eyes and saw a rainbow of colours flashing around her. The bright lights looked like the most amazing firework display.

Then, just like that, she found herself on solid ground – Fairyland ground.

She sucked in a breath. Honeysuckle adored living in the Bigs' world, helping to keep nature safe. It was a huge world full of mystery, where she never quite knew what would happen next.

There had been times in the past when she'd been so clumsy that Mother Nature had almost sent her

back to Fairyland, and the thought
of leaving her friends behind had
filled her with horror. But she had to
admit, Fairyland did
look incredibly
magical.

There were turquoise toadstools dotted through creamy candyfloss fields, and the sun in the sky shone different colours, depending on the time of day. Right now, it was a very pale pink, casting a beautiful dusky light everywhere.

There were lots of fairies flying around, going about their business. Many of them smiled at her, but no one stopped to talk. Everyone was so busy – they had a job to do.

She thought of her friends back in the Bigs' world. They'd all found their purpose and got their wings and jobs, too, yet here she was, still without either. Maybe she just wasn't good enough to be any kind of fairy. Perhaps she really would be the first fairy never to get her wings. She felt sick at the thought.

"At least I've got you, Pip," she

said, trying to make herself feel better. She bent down to stroke her dragling, who was prodding her nose into the backs of Honeysuckle's knees.

She'd almost forgotten why she was here, and told herself off for being selfish. She had to find Mother Nature! Honeysuckle started running along the shiny, glass-cobbled streets, and Pip scampered behind her. Mother Nature would be easy to spot, surely?

After passing the candyfloss fields, Honeysuckle turned into a wide park full of lollipop trees. She looked down at the ground – it wasn't

made of grass but hundreds of gold and silver stars, like a spectacular, shimmering carpet.

Honeysuckle began to ask other fairies if they'd seen Mother Nature. She managed to stop a Seasons Fairy, who had hair like icicles and wings to match. "No, I'm sorry," the fairy replied. The Seasons Fairy dashed off with her ice-white dragling at her heels.

A Seed Fairy said the same thing, and so did a Moon Fairy. As Honeysuckle stepped out of the park and onto a street that glittered like red rubies, she was starting to feel stupid. Mother Nature did a very important job and was busy looking after the whole world – both Fairyland and the Bigs' world. Honeysuckle was silly to think she could find her here so easily!

The sun had turned a beautiful lilac by now, and Honeysuckle knew she should be getting back. She was angry at herself for wasting so much time in Fairyland when she could have been helping in the Bigs' world. But just as she stopped by a firelight hedgerow, about to wish herself back, she heard a shout.

"Honeysuckle, is that you?"

Honeysuckle spun round. Billow, one of the Cloud Fairies that she knew from the Bigs' world, was flying towards her. "Oh, hi, Billow," she said. "I… I was looking for Mother Nature," she explained.

"I'm not sure you'll find her here,"

Billow said, with a swing of her curly white hair. "She's been very busy in the Bigs' world today." As she spoke, a few more Cloud Fairies gathered around her with their draglings.

"I know," Honeysuckle said. "I'd actually given up on finding

Mother Nature here. I was just about to head home."

"We are too," said Droplet, another of the Cloud Fairies.

Her transparent wings looked like shimmering drops of water. "We've just been to visit some of our Dream Fairy friends, over on Jewel Mountain, but it's time to get back to our cloud duties!"

"I think we'll do a sprinkle of rain tonight, just to cool things down after another hot summer's day," said Billow. "We'll see you back at the Fairythorn Tree!"

"Wait!" Honeysuckle had just had an idea. It might be a bit crazy – but it was worth a try. Maybe she could save the bees after all!

Chapter 8

Honeysuckle was bursting with impatience on the journey back to the Bigs' world. The invisible roundabout spun down and down, the magical rainbow colours flashing around her and Pip. It was a beautiful sight, but all she wanted was to get back quickly so she could put her plan into action.

As soon as Honeysuckle felt her feet hit the grassy ground, she glanced about, looking for transport.

Billow and Droplet had promised they'd gather as many Cloud Fairies as they could manage. But for Honeysuckle's plan to work they'd need a lot – she'd have to do her bit too. The problem was that Cloud Fairies spent almost all their time in the sky, so she'd need help to fly around in order to track them down.

"Hey, Honeysuckle, there you are," said a voice above her. "We've been wondering where you'd got to!"

It was Posy, zooming down to the ground. As soon as she landed, she took off her purple headdress, shook out her black hair, then positioned the headdress back on her head.

"I've been to Fairyland, actually," Honeysuckle admitted. "But there's no time to talk about that now. I need your help."

Soon, all three of Honeysuckle's best friends were passing on her message to any Cloud Fairy they could find. Honeysuckle hitched a ride on the back of a very kind blackbird, and they flew through the clouds spreading word of Honeysuckle's plan. Yet again, she wished she didn't have to rely on other animals all the time. Even if they were incredibly generous, like this blackbird, or the ants from earlier.

There wasn't much time before sunset, and Honeysuckle and her friends gathered together at the foot of the Fairythorn Tree, their draglings playing in the moss patch nearby. "Everything's almost ready," Honeysuckle said. "The Cloud Fairies are in place. There's just one thing left to do."

"What's that?" asked Rose, as a dazed bee buzzed towards her shoulder, spun round, and then flew off again. "We haven't got long until the Bigs go to bed, and then before long it'll be morning and we might be too late to save the bees." Rose's pale face looked even paler than usual.

"For the plan to work properly we need the little Big's help," Honeysuckle said. "Do you think that will be okay, Rose? It *is* an emergency."

Rose put her hands to her face, and then nodded.

"Whatever we need to do," Fleur said, her eyes flashing all the colours of the rainbow. "I'll do it!"

Honeysuckle smiled. Fleur was

certainly the most daring of all of them. She told Fleur the plan.

Posy, Rose, Honeysuckle and their four draglings huddled underneath a large stone toadstool near the Miller's back door. From there they watched Fleur

as she fluttered up to the windowsill.

"Be careful," Rose whispered.

Alice was in the kitchen, doing the drying up. Honeysuckle had remembered that the little Big sometimes had toast for her supper, but the toaster often got stuck. It usually ended up with a really awful bell sound ringing for ages, and Mr and Mrs Miller flapping about with teacloths and opening all the windows and doors. That was exactly what Honeysuckle needed to happen tonight!

Honeysuckle's heart hammered

in her chest as Fleur tapped on the kitchen window. The fairies saw the little Big jump back in surprise, and then a beaming smile break out on her face. "A fairy!" she mouthed.

Even though Fleur was too far away and had her back to the fairies, Honeysuckle knew what she would be saying. She'd be asking Alice to make herself some toast, but make sure it got stuck.

Honeysuckle held Rose and Posy's hands as they waited for Alice's reply. The little Big had opened the window, and her head poked out of the gap. Honeysuckle suddenly realised how much danger she'd put her friend into. With one swipe of the little Big's hand, Fleur could be gone!

She was about to shout out for Fleur to get away, when Alice nodded and started opening a loaf of bread on the worktop. Fleur had done it! The fairy spun round on the window sill and dived down to the ground. She flapped her white wings only at the very last minute – just as if she were playing fairy bungee.

The three fairies gave Fleur a giant hug as she joined them under the toadstool. "You were brilliant!" Honeysuckle said.

The plan to save the bees was in place. Now all the fairies could do was hope that it worked.

Chapter 9

The sun was beginning to glow red above the horizon – sunset wasn't too far away. The fairies had already put the word out that all the animals and wildlife should take shelter tonight. Although of course they couldn't do anything about the bees, who were still buzzing around the garden in a daze.

Honeysuckle's head throbbed. She felt very nervous. What if things didn't go as planned? The bees wouldn't just be confused then – they be gone altogether!

Honeysuckle looked up at the Cloud Fairies who had gathered on the top branches of the Fairythorn Tree, waiting for Honeysuckle's sign. There were hundreds of them, all with beautiful wings in a variety of shades of white, grey and blue. Together, they looked like a flock of tiny birds.

But Honeysuckle couldn't give the sign yet. She was relying on the little Big first. She hoped that Alice would go through with the plan. She knew the little Big liked the fairies – she'd been kind and given them presents in the past. But today was about more than just being kind.

"Are you sure she said yes, Fleur?" Honeysuckle asked, frowning. "She seems to be taking a long time."

"As sure as I am that birds can sing!" Fleur said, nodding her star-dusted red curls.

Rose put her arm around Honeysuckle. "It's a great plan," she said. "We've just got to be patient."

Honeysuckle smiled. Rose was always good at making her feel better.

But she still dashed over to the other side of the toadstool and looked up anxiously at the Bigs' kitchen window.

What was happening? If Alice didn't carry out her part of the plan soon, Honeysuckle would just have to signal to the Cloud Fairies anyway, and hope that doing half the plan would still work!

Beeeeeeep! Beeeeeeep! Beeeeeeep! Beeeeeeep! Beeeeeeep! Beeeeeeep!

The four fairies stuck their fingers in their pointy ears and the draglings huddled into each other to block out the sound.

The noise was awful! Like a deafening crow's caw right beside them – but a thousand times worse. Still, Honeysuckle's heart leapt with joy. The little Big had done it! Alice was pushing open the back door and the kitchen window, while Mrs Miller was in the living room, opening the patio doors.

"For goodness sake, Alice! You burned the toast *again*!" she heard the Big shout as the smoke alarm continued.

"Sorry Mum, but it always gets stuck!" Alice called back.

The fairies could see the little Big upstairs now, opening the skylight and then her bedroom window.

Honeysuckle had to act quickly. She ran back to the other side of the toadstool.

"Give me a hand up, could you?" she said to her friends.

This was something they used

to do all the time, before any of them got their wings. Fleur and Posy held their hands out so that Honeysuckle could step into their palms. From there she jumped up onto the top of the toadstool. She scrambled up on the shiny red paint and pushed herself to standing. Then she waved both arms in the air.

Honeysuckle squinted up at the Cloud Fairies, hoping they had seen her. Yes! They swarmed up, higher and higher, circling like one great fluttering cloud. Then, beneath them, dark grey clouds started appearing from nowhere, and soon Honeysuckle couldn't see the Cloud Fairies at all. The grey sky loomed above, and Honeysuckle realised she needed to get back under the toadstool, fast!

She sat down and slid off the edge, jumping down to the ground without worrying about the drop — she'd made plenty of big jumps just like this one when she danced.

As she landed, she felt a big drop of rain on her head, and dashed in towards the toadstool's stalk. Her friends were huddled together, staring out into the garden. Honeysuckle

turned round and followed their gaze.
Huge raindrops were pouring down,
splashing as they hit the ground.
Bounce, bounce, bounce! The rain
filled the garden. It was like being in
the middle of a Big-sized fountain!

By now, the dreadful ringing

from the Bigs' house had stopped. Instead, Mrs Miller was shrieking at the top of her voice, "Eeeeek, the rain! The house is getting completely drenched!"

Chapter 10

The four fairies wiped the splashes from their arms and legs as they peeked out from the toadstool. The rain had stopped just as suddenly as it had started, but the garden looked absolutely soaked. The grass was sparkling with water in the remaining sunlight, and the pond was brimming over, with water flowing across the flagstones around it.

Even though the fairies were far

away from the pond, they could hear Clive and Derek complaining.

"First wind, and now this terrible rain!"

"I bet it's got something to do with those pesky fairies. Eugh, it's even got under my hat!"

"If I wasn't made of concrete I'd be shivering. Somebody get us a towel!"

Honeysuckle tried to ignore them. They'd be fine, really – and she was much more worried about the bees! But where were they? She rushed out and looked up at the Bigs' house, then up at the bees' hive in the Fairythorn Tree, then back to the house again.

Wait – what was that? Yes, there was a bee flying out of the little Big's bedroom window. And there was another. Honeysuckle dropped her gaze down, and saw at least ten bees buzzing out of the patio doors. She pulled Rose's arm. "Has it worked?" she asked.

"I think so!" Rose replied.

"You've done it!" Fleur and Posy said in unison.

The fairies watched, beaming,

as bees all over the garden seemed to wake up from their daze. The ones that had got lost in the grass were buzzing up towards their hive, and bees kept on streaming out of the Bigs' house from the open windows.

Honeysuckle's plan had worked! The downpour of rain had cleared the air of the nasty spray that had affected the bees. Most importantly, it had saved all the bees in the house, because so much rain had got in through the doors and windows! The bees had come to their senses, and were no longer confused.

Honeysuckle felt a glow of happiness spread through her from head to toe.

"That was brilliant, Honeysuckle," Posy said. "You're so clever!"

The fairies joined in a group hug with their draglings squirming in the middle, then Honeysuckle felt a tap on her shoulder. She turned round to see Billow.

"Did it work okay?" she asked, her face tight with concern.

"Perfectly," smiled Honeysuckle. "Thank you so much for all your help."

Billow grinned, her icicle-blue

eyes crinkling at the corners. "No problem – any time! Now, I'd better get back – more clouds and a drizzle of rain are due tomorrow."

"The draglings will be happy about that," Posy said. "They've been getting really hot and bothered in the heat recently."

"Please send our thanks to all the Cloud Fairies," said Honeysuckle.

"I will!" Billow called as she fluttered up towards the clouds once more.

"We should get back to helping with the pollinating," said

Honeysuckle, grabbing her basket from under the toadstool. "There's a little light before sunset, and the bees still need our help to catch up."

Just as the fairies were about to leave, the little Big leapt out of her back door. The fairies backed away under the toadstool to hide again.

Alice's long damp hair swung about as she skipped around the sodden garden. The fairies could hear the grass squelching under her bare feet, but the little Big didn't seem to care. "Fairies, fairies!" she called. "Where are you?"

Honeysuckle held her breath as Alice scampered towards the toadstool. The little Big stopped right beside the ornament and crouched down in the rain-soaked grass. The fairies could see her sparkly pink toenails and her purple leggings that were splashed with rain. Honeysuckle widened her eyes at her friends. The little Big was so close!

The fairies couldn't see Alice's face, but they could hear her talking in a soft voice.

"Fairy, I know you're there," she whispered. "I hope the bees are safe now. My mum was mad at me for burning the toast and then the rain coming in everywhere, but I hope I helped you."

Fleur tugged on Rose's elbow, and Posy hid her head under her arm. None of the fairies dared to reply. Honeysuckle sucked in a breath as the little Big's toes started to wiggle. Was she leaving?

Then a giant hand appeared on the ground right next to the toadstool, cupped palm up. The fairies stared at it, transfixed. What was the little Big doing?

"I wanted to give you a present, and I guessed you like bees..." Alice said.

Honeysuckle looked closer. In the middle of the little Big's hand was a golden bee on a metal hook.

"I lost the other earring ages ago, so I thought you might like the this one." The little Big's hand turned sideways to tip the earring onto the ground. It was very pretty and shiny – just the sort of thing that fairies loved!

The grass rustled as the little Big stood up. Alice squelched back towards the house and Honeysuckle crept over to the edge of the toadstool. "Thank you!" she whispered shyly. She couldn't help it.

The little Big swung her head round, and Honeysuckle watched as the corners of her mouth turned up into a huge grin. Then she turned back, and bounced into the house.

Chapter 11

"I really should go and check on the bees!" Honeysuckle said. She called to Pip and scanned the garden for some transport.

"And I've got to go and get ready for the Sunset Song." Fleur's white wings shimmered as she fluttered up into the air.

"We'll go and carry on with the pollination," said Rose, linking one arm with Posy and swinging her basket on the other.

"See you at sunset!" Posy said. The two friends zoomed up into the sky, their draglings darting about in the air behind them.

Honeysuckle spotted the kind blackbird who'd helped her earlier, and waved. Soon she was on her way up to the bees' nest, with the beautiful gold earring safely in her straw basket.

The fairy carefully slid off the bird's feathery back onto a branch next to the bees. "Thank you, blackbird," she said. "Will you wait for just a moment?"

"Certainly," the bird replied in a twittering, tuneful voice. "It'd be my pleasure."

Honeysuckle edged along the wet tree branch, with Pip right behind her. She got to the opening of the bees' nest and very slowly poked her head in. The bees looked so much happier, buzzing around normally and making their honey.

"Hello bees, are you all okay?" Honeysuckle asked.

"We're fine now, thank you, fairy," said one close by.

"It's like we've woken up from a

dream," buzzed another.

"Will you be able to get back to the pollinating now?" Honeysuckle asked. "There's still a little time before sunset."

In answer, hundreds of the bees flew to the front of the nest.

"Of course," a smaller, younger bee said. "We'd forgotten before, but now we know what to do."

"Then follow me," Honeysuckle called, running back along the branch and jumping onto the blackbird. They took off, followed by a swarm of bees, and Honeysuckle asked the blackbird

to land in the flower beds by the patio.
There was still lots of pollen to collect
there.

The bees buzzed and squeaked in
happiness as they flew from flower to
flower, doing the job they were so good

at. Honeysuckle hoped they would still be able to get all the pollinating done – she knew how important it was to keep the flowers and plants growing in the garden.

She skipped and danced about, encouraging the bees from flower to flower. She twirled around in a patch of lavender and beckoned over a trio of bees to some pretty ballerina fuchsias that were full of pollen. Honeysuckle absently scratched at her back as she leaped and pirouetted.

She felt something brush against her hair, and bounced round. But it wasn't a worker bee, as she'd expected, it was the Queen Bee!

"Sorry to make you jump," the Queen Bee said in a light, musical voice. "I called your name, but you were so busy with the pollinating I don't think you heard."

Honeysuckle was shocked – the Queen Bee almost never left her nest. What was she doing here? "H-hello," she stuttered. "Is everything okay?" She curtsied low among the lavender.

"Very much so," the Queen Bee replied. "I wanted to thank you in person for your hard work and clever thinking. You saved my bees, and for that I will be eternally grateful."

Honeysuckle felt her cheeks redden. She was almost speechless. "It… it was nothing, really," she managed. "I'm just glad the bees are well again."

"They most certainly are," said the Queen Bee. "They will be able to finish pollinating now – Mother Nature can be sure of that."

The fairy beamed, and felt a flush of happiness, which suddenly turned into a buzzing, tingling feeling all over her back. The tingles prickled at her back like pins and needles, and Honeysuckle felt heat flood her body. Then the sound of tiny bells rang in her ears and Honeysuckle was covered in a cloud of fairy dust. Her wings! They had unfurled like golden leaves, bright yellow with sparkling white tips.

"They're beautiful," said the

Queen Bee. "My congratulations, Honeysuckle. I always knew you'd be a Pollen Fairy, even if you didn't!"

"Thank you!" Honeysuckle said, doing another curtsey. Then, without even thinking about it, her legs carried her off to dance among the flowers again.

Honeysuckle's new wings glimmered gold with fairy magic as she bounced and twirled around. She gave them a little flutter, then another. Soon she was flying about the flower bed, soaring gracefully from bloom to bloom.

Chapter 12

Honeysuckle sat on her scallop-shell bed, stroking Pip. Her dragling had turned the most glorious shade of yellow, just like a buttercup, with brilliant white paws, nose and tail.

This was the colour Pip w o u l d stay for ever — as soon as a

fairy's wings unfurled, their dragling changed to their permanent colour. Pip looked very pleased as she flicked her tail about beside her Pollen fairy.

"I'm so happy you've got your wings, Honeysuckle," said Fleur from the pine-cone chair. She'd just returned from a particularly spectacular Sunset Song. It was so magical and tuneful, even the butterflies had clapped in delight.

"They're simply gorgeous," said Posy. "Tomorrow I'll make you a headdress to match!"

The fairies were resting in

Honeysuckle's new bedroom after a very busy day. Secretly, Honeysuckle was dying to go outside and try out her wings again, but she didn't want to be rude and throw her friends out of her room.

"Ahh, you hung up the bee!" Rose noticed. "It goes perfectly there."

Honeysuckle had used the hook part of the earring to hang the bee to the right of the window. "It looks great, doesn't it?" she agreed, smiling.

"What's that?" Fleur said, jumping up. Outside, the wind was swirling again. Honeysuckle dashed over to the knothole window. *Please don't let it be Grot Goblins again!* she thought.

All four fairies poked their heads out of the window, trying to work out what was happening. Leaves swirled around the garden, and then started to circle up towards the window. Honeysuckle gasped as they formed a face – it was a message from Mother Nature!

"I would like to say thank you, Honeysuckle," the leaves rustled out the words. "You did something wonderful today in saving the bees."

Honeysuckle gave a shy little smile. "That's very kind, Mother Nature," she said quietly. "But I couldn't have done it without the kindness of others – like the Cloud Fairies, and my friends here, and a lovely blackbird and an army of ants."

Mother Nature nodded. "You're right – it's important for everyone to work together in this world," she said. "And I'm delighted to see you have found your purpose – congratulations on your wings. You're a natural Pollen Fairy, and you should be very proud."

Honeysuckle's smile turned into

a giant beam. She squeezed out of the window and took off into the air, eager to show Mother Nature her unfurled wings. Soon the other three fairies had darted through the window too. They flew about together among the Fairythorn branches, while Mother Nature's leafy face looked on in pride.

"I must go now, fairies," she said. "Don't stay up too late – it's been a long and tiring day for you all."

The leaves began swirling again. A moment later, Mother Nature's face had gone.

"How about a quick game of

fairy bungee before bedtime?" Fleur suggested.

"Ooh, yes, please!" Honeysuckle cried, flying up to the branch above.

The fairies lined up on the branch, and Honeysuckle grinned with happiness.

"One, two, three, go!" announced Rose. The four fairies sprang off the branch and dived downwards like shooting stars, the air rushing past them as they went.

Honeysuckle saw the ground coming up towards her and shook out her wings. She swished them hard in the air and swooped upwards, left and then right and then left again. Now she'd got her wings, Honeysuckle felt as if she could do anything. She was a real fairy – a Pollen Fairy – after all!

Rose

Rose is kind, sensitive and gentle. She's always trying to make things better for those around her, but is also a worrier. She likes sparkly things, flower petals and weaving decorations into her hair.

Posy

Posy is unstoppable and brave. She adores animals and is often found riding butterflies or chatting to squirrels. Posy loves to wear feathers and her clothes are mainly assembled from things she finds in nature.

Honeysuckle

Honeysuckle is a dreamer. She's a bit dizzy and clumsy, but very sweet with it. She has boundless energy and loves to dance among the flowers, releasing their scent as she pirouettes from bloom to bloom.

Fleur

Fleur is feisty, funny, fiery and cool. Her striking red hair twinkles with tiny stars and her eyes are always changing colour. She loves music and singing. Fleur can make a musical instrument from anything she finds, especially natural things.

Collect them all!

Rose and the
Friendship Wish
ISBN 978-1-84877-968-6

Posy and the
Trouble with Draglings
ISBN 978-1-84877-970-9

Fleur and the
Sunset Chorus
ISBN 978-1-84877-972-3

Honeysuckle
and the Bees
ISBN 978-1-84877-969-3